JUDGE'S COMMENTS FOR
How The Garden Looks From Here

In Lisa Zimmerman's poems there is much sorrow, often hinted and muted, but there is more joy, spoken and sung. The speaker in these poems loves her children, the sky, the lake, and her horses. She lives in the world as if it's the only one; the things of her life matter—the worth of each blade of grass, each bird, each dream, each word is tangible, weighted, and given to us in a poetry measured and strong. These poems know that the truths of our lives, or that which is as close to truth as our words and wisdom get, lie in the specific, the attention to detail—frozen wash on the line, the mare in the field, the young daughter's coming into the world where the dinosaurs are all dead, but there's nothing we can do to bring them back, nothing we can do at all except learn that "what we love/moves on... long before we ever hold it in our arms." In this first full-length collection, Zimmerman promises us more to come, a garden of riches, a voice that renders the livable world into usable wisdom.

—Rick Campbell, *Anhingha Press*

HOW THE GARDEN LOOKS FROM HERE

BY LISA ZIMMERMAN

Snake Nation Press
Valdosta, GA
2004

Snake Nation Press
wishes to thank the
Price Campbell Foundation
Barbara Passmore

Published by Snake Nation Press
110 West Force Street
Valdosta, Georgia 31601
www.snakenationpress.org

Editors:
Roberta George
Jean Arambula

ISBN 0-9754843-2-X

Special thanks to my sister Diane, my children Sylvan, Avalon and Arthur, and to these poets and friends who have inspired and supported me over the years: Melissa Katsimpalis, Veronica Patterson, Kathy Willard, Jack Martin, James Tipton, Michele Barnett, Wendy Berger, Larry Scott, Julie Foster, Lisa Sarkis Neaville, Bill W., Janie Hinds, George Kalamaras, James Grabill, and John Bradley. A heartfelt thank you to my husband John, who always believed.

for John

TABLE OF CONTENTS

How The Garden Looks From Here

PART ONE

There are days we live
as if death were nowhere
in the background.
—*Li-Young Lee*

MARKETPLACE

Someone is always trying to sell something.
The men are impatient and hot
and want to be somewhere else.
I pay for earrings sworn to be silver.
But they are too light in my ears
and glint like lies in the noon sun.

Bargaining is hard business
so I go where the women are
sitting among baskets and bright blankets,
motionless beneath whirling fans.
I am lulled by their voices, soft gossip,
the whisper of embroidered cotton dresses.

The women have cool brown hands
that lift my baby into shade
where their own children string shells
the color of watermelon and fresh mangos.
It is easy to be here.

I carry things around: a purse, a ring,
a marble bird. I put things back, deciding.
There is so much time for hesitation.
The heat does not find us here.

The women share the baby between them
like a ripe fruit. Outside a man is shouting.
All around us the children play and laugh
and grow up suddenly
right in the middle of our lives.

PASSAGE

Each morning my mother awakens
into her unknown body.
Slippers fall quiet but hard across the carpet
down the hall to the kitchen.
Pots clang in my sleep at the outer edge of the house.
I hear my sister breathing.

My mother cooks well and claims to love the art,
hours around the stove and refrigerator,
chop, mince, dice, fry.
My father eats like a king and thrives.
I push food around the plate's white circle
trying to break the code.
My mother shouts: "It's not poison! Eat!"
The papery potatoes, peas glistening in butter,
the beef from butcher to table.
My mother's mute and angry communion: We eat to live.
My sister's dark eyes wait for my translation.

At night in bed food burns into dreams.
Bread is wood I build a ladder with rung by rung.
My sister waits for wind to rush down the hole I search for.
Our mother in a dark room grinds her teeth.

THE HOUSE IN MASNUY ST. JEAN, BELGIUM

What I couldn't bear was its old stone, its red brick,
its tiny country windows set in their deep cool basins,
how shade from the yard pressed and entered
from the back through the kitchen
where Arlette ironed linen tablecloths and lace curtains,
the iron hissing weary steam.
I couldn't bear the white-faced cows scattered
along the muddy road and horses, content and lovely,
tearing green weeds beside those wired fields.
I couldn't bear the lush grass my brother mowed and mowed
how cheerfully it grew around the dirt-filled well with its belch
of gaudy roses. I couldn't bear
my brother falling into bed another night
unable to form a single syllable of despair
or how my own bedroom window creaked open
when I slipped out onto the moon-drenched patio
past the room holding the snoring Colonel
asleep beside his drunk and bitter wife.

ONE OF THE FIRST SUMMERS

1.

We were unprepared that year
for the sun's fierce burn
wasting everything green in our garden.
We watched green shoots struggle
only to shrink into cracked ground,
the baked and brittle leaves, squash scarce on spindly vines.

But the baby tumbled inside
and I grew taut as a melon.
In spite of drought
and all the seeds that never germinated
a world trembled into being.

2.

Each year brings a new lesson in change.
And we who were not talking,
we who had not talked for so long
took ourselves into the garden.
While the baby crept through tickling grass
you raked and combed our bit of earth.
My hands between rows of rampant beans
pulled bright, tiny weeds that shot up,
like our daughter, a sign that all things thrive.

How I See It

for my sister

When the baby fell two feet
onto asphalt and I lifted him
and saw the blood stream down his face
like some great tear
I carried him as I carried you
running for our lives
through the long corridor of our childhood.
Only this is in the Home
we've just delivered our grandmother from
and I'm dodging wheelchairs where women
lean forward over slack hands,
hands that once held babies
just like this one, my last.
He's screaming and I'm racing,
breath jerking in and out of my chest,
blood splashing onto his hands, my shirt,
I'm searching for a nurse, I say help me
because I don't know how bad it is, this damage.
I didn't know with you either,
only that you were younger than I was
and it was like a war.
I had to get us out alive.

How a Sliver of Purple Far Away Became
My Daughter Running Toward Me

At the mall in the glitter,
the noise of merchandise rubbing against itself
and hands touching the merchandise,
I suddenly heard the quiet
of one child missing
and for five minutes
or a long, terrible lifetime
I did not see that child anywhere—
her long red hair, the purple sweatsuit
and all the bangles she'd put on before we left home,
strings and strings of plastic beads, and the ring
with one green stone on her index finger, right hand,
the finger with the brown freckle
oh, the panic
drove deep into my body as I walked
through the shop to its mouth yawning into the mall,
the baby on one hip, the older girl's thin hand in mine,
and I could see in all the faces moving by
that no one cared about my life at all
so I looked first one direction, then the other,
my eyes assaulted by glare and glass,
the shiny updated decor, tile and indoor plants
shooting up to skylights and I simply
screamed her name.

MIDDLE CHILD

Dawn rolls over the house, hot and filled.
Only the middle child is awake.

I hear her land on the carpet from her high bed.
Soon she will look for me and find me here, like faith.

She will tell me the story she read before sleeping
about the Chinese girl too poor to buy a paintbrush

who is given a magic brush in a dream.
The beggar girl paints a bird that flies up

and sings, a fish who flips his tail
and leaps into the pond.

My girl's eyes will be solemn when she tells me this.
We will sit silently together in shared reverence.

Until then I wait in this separate room, listening to her
quiet movements, a drawer sliding, words spoken to the dozing cat.

The tall sister stretches in her cloudless sleep.
The brother climbs across his last dream

running toward daylight. From my past
where my mother is drinking in the dark

and my father is asleep in his life,
I painted these children.

Night Light

I leave a light on in the kitchen each night.
It stretches out across the cool stove,

a luminous wing growing brighter while we sleep.
I have wakened to my name called,

moved through the pillowed dark
and felt a hand guide me

down the hallway to rooms where children
toss in their blanket boats

and the small one reaches out to be rescued.
As I walk our bodies back through the hush,

the hand sifts light in the kitchen
and the ancestors, the great grandmothers,

lean on counters, talking softly among themselves.
I know then how the light spreads its fingers

through such a big house
and why the boy, heavy in my arms,
is not afraid when he wakes.

TOMATOES

All summer I wait
for tomatoes to ripen.
I dream of their fat globes,
seeds trapped in a red sea,
thin-skinned and drenched in yellow sunlight.

August beats the ground dry.
Suddenly I see there are too many.
They drop plump and hot into my hands.
I pick and pick until my fingers stain
and the heavy fruit roll from the basket
to splatter and bleed at my feet.

Impatience is resistance to learning, I have heard.
In the heated kitchen I stir and salt and taste,
add basil, thyme, crushed garlic.
My daughter, clutching my leg, cries, "Up, Mama, up!"
I lift her warm damp body to mine.
The boiling pasta overflows.
Autumn slides down the mountain uninvited
while we sleep. I wake alarmed and ask
what else have I forgotten, what else?

ON THE BEACH, CANCUN

Out on this edge of land
my daughter rebuilds
the ruins.
I see her blonde head bobbing, a mirage
she springs from the turquoise water.

At times the rush of surf
frightens her. She runs up
the wet hill of sand
and back down again
with new courage.

My daughter tells me
she loves the world
and pats it with her red shovel.
She thinks stars fall at night
to live again as tiny creatures
saved by the water's terrible grace.
Beside her in a bucket
swim broken and maimed bits of ocean.
They find their way to her small hands
and are blessed and made beautiful.

For days she wore only the aqua sweatshirt
spaghetti stained with grimy cuffs,
the brontosaurus beaming out at us from her chest
the words EXTINCT IS FOREVER, which she cannot read,
floating below his happy face.
He is her friend,
she wears him like an emblem
through the lacquered afternoon
stomping through the house, her private rain forest.
And we know as we watch her
that she expects to spot him at any time
around some corner, in the garden, or at least at the zoo
where surely all creatures are saved and celebrated.
How she would pat and embrace him
her hand a white leaf against his skin.
She would feed him bits of bread, rice, sliced banana, anything
to see him tremble with joy
down the length of his great uncomplicated body.

Then one morning she approached us
just risen from sleep and said All the dinosaurs died
with a grief so deep and pure we could only
nod and apologize and regret—
she learned so soon that what we love
moves on sometimes across the dreamy landscape
long before we ever hold it in our arms.

He is holding her so tenderly
like his own daughter
her small naked body folding
over his arm like white laundry.
He has carried her from smoke and flames,
streaked with soot she is pressed against his slicker,
her small head thrown back, her blonde hair tangled
where his massive gloved hand barely touches
and he is blowing into the little *O* of her mouth,
his big heart beating against her narrow chest
where her lungs, those tiny cellophane sacs are, please,
filling with air again.
And what I need to know is that she woke
sleepy as a newborn, looked up
into that great brown face,
saw the dark holy eyes of God
or anybody's father
and knew she was saved.

The Wash Prayer

On the best days I offer
this invisible work, this work
so easily undone.
So when the memory of sleep
is smoothed from beds,
when breakfast bowls return
to their cupboard I begin
the litany of laundry
sadly astonished to see again
the hill of clothes slumped
in the wicker basket,
all their pride gone, their lives
inhabiting other garments.
And if it's a good day I lovingly
sort dark socks and wadded trousers
from the baby's white T-shirts
and his sisters' pastels.
Into the vessel, faithful as a truck,
they go, to churn and swirl
in their mysterious froth
making shapes I cannot see.
And after the dryer revives
each wet skin I sit
and fold these clothes into
safety, health, laughter,
home.

WHEN GOD MADE THE BABY

He was tired so mistakes were inevitable.
The heart was missing valves and was programmed
to beat for only four months.
The eyes were blind but large and beautiful
so the parents could look deep into them
but the baby could only see a futureless wall.

God made the ears into odd ornaments
placed low on the baby's head, with no abilities at all.
He did not want the baby to hear the parents crying.

God made the little stomach a separate place
that did not connect upward
though kind and skillful doctors would make adjustments.

God drew simple maps in the baby's brain
with blue crayon, knowing
the baby wouldn't need to learn
difficult, useless things like algebra, or driving a car,
or swallowing.

Just before placing the tiny fetus into the woman
God pulled on the baby's arm, stretching it like bread dough.
When the baby rushed out of the woman's body
into hospital daylight, everyone could see God
would take the baby by that long arm
and yank him back whenever He felt like it.

SEWING BATMAN'S CAPE
AFTER THE FUNERAL OF A FRIEND'S SON

So simple but it's taking me all day
to move the black silk fabric
under the little foot of the machine,
my son sweeping in and out of the room
in his red socks, asking again
if I'm done with it, if it's finished yet
and I am already exhausted by the dark
folds in my lap, the needle piercing
the cloth over and over, the cloth giving in
to the tiny black stitches following
endlessly one after another, the day loosening itself
around the house, my boy is so pleased
when the cape is finally tied around his neck,
how he runs in and out of each room, leaping
from beds, the couch, the chairs, shouting
for me to watch how it flies
behind him so black and shiny,
so real.

The Night After the Partial Eclipse

I gave it my best, found two pieces of cardboard,
made a hole in one, covered it with tinfoil,
pierced a smaller hole in that but it didn't matter
how I maneuvered each piece
we just couldn't see it happen as it happened
and my older girl, wrought with disappointment,
would have looked directly at the waning sun if I hadn't stopped her.

But later, when the children each fell into that other shadow,
I sat outside and saw the moon, faithless tramp,
hanging next to Venus, over the lake, no less.
And together they beamed, one a brilliant gaudy scrap of light,
the other half dressed, dangling her beaded rope across the water,
begging, I suppose, for the usual forgiveness.

What Is the Weight of a Boy's Grief?

Is it heavier than the night quilt a father pulls back?
Heavier than the words his mouth must form,
the small cold stones a river offers?

Is it more than the weight of the coffin hoisted
onto the backs of eight silent men
chosen for the honor of carrying her body
away from the boy?
More than each man grasping the shoulder
of the man across from him, beneath the casket,
as if to say Brother, help me to do this
and I will help you to do this.

How much does a boy's grief weigh?
More than the black suit holding his shoulders steady.
More than the broken wing of his man's heart.
More than the dirt weeping out of his hand.

PAST LIVES

Not the Crusades or World Wars,
not Korea or Vietnam
but some unholy virus
has seized our boy on the naked beach
of his eighth year and it holds him
in a cell we cannot enter.
He is fevered and wild
and keeps invisible enemies at bay
with his bare hands.
You tell him you are his father
but it doesn't matter.
The small hanger of his shoulders lifts—
he is focused and angry, upright
but still sleeping
and he's out to kill you, too.

Our son told me a dream
he once had. He was
a knight among many knights
on a high castle wall.
and was pierced by an arrow
and fell and fell and fell.
He was just like the rest of us:
a slave, a carrier of rock, servant
to some diseased king.

At the hospital the doctors are bright
foolish men in white coats.
But I love them for their kindness.
It is the only real food we have
at this moment.
I'm thinking of someone's daughter
who, at ten, one day in June,
could not walk straight.
She died in October.

It is still October.

Untethered Time

The hour is day broken over blue ice
The hour of three boys pulling an old sled
The hour with dishes in the sink and three boys
and a ragged white wind lassoed by the window
The hour it takes to come up for air
This breathing hour
The hour of difficult gratitude
The hour fills with the dog's large barking
and three boys and the sled's wooden scrape
Slow slow
The hour fills with wet boots and socks and black paws
The hour is a holy moment
The hour is gratitude difficult
Full of wind
And coming up for air

SOME OF THE WAYS I SEE HOW YOU GOT WHERE YOU ARE
for Sylvan

It was May.
It was autumn.
It was a wedding.
It was the thin gloss of the egg come down,
unhindered.
It was a reasonable distance.
Blankets over the window, zero
degree dawn, people had hands like
gloved flowers.
Then it was a house with a woodstove.
Later a house with a wooden fence.
Your head in a book, the book
with a tiger in it. A sister. A brother.
Later it was a pair of red Converse sneakers, no laces.
The soft geometry of a body growing while sleeping.
It took years. It was yesterday. Outside
behind the house the lake is
sometimes the color of your eyes.
Sometimes not.

ARTHUR AND HIS SISTER

The girl who always wanted a brother
steers him now in the red canoe.
It edges from shore
and slips onto the sky
which the lake holds up
in its silver mirror.

The boy does not know
if he is a king but he feels royal
in the eyes of this sister.
And although she does not look like
a priestess in her baseball cap
she rows steadily, her long hair
a fountain of light down her back,
the boat skimming the wet scarf of sky.

This is not legend yet. There has been no battle,
no betrayal, no regret.
But it's as if the girl is taking
the young king home to be mended,
the boat gently rocking,
oars dipping into the clouds, into the sun.

Part Two

I think it was from the animals
that St. Francis learned
it is possible to cast yourself
on the earth's good mercy and live.
—Jane Hirshfield

HOW THE GARDEN LOOKS FROM HERE
for Donna

The cat finds her way among herbs
while bees follow each other into an audience

of blossoms. Already a door on the house
has opened into sunlight and a woman

sits at a wheel and shapes a bowl
from a flake of earth. The dog yawns

beside her, waiting. No one notices
the horses moving, slow as stars,

across the dry grass
of sky.

THE WIND, THE LAKE, THE DEER

What is wind? the way it spends itself
against the house, sleeps briefly
like a child in fever, then wakes afraid
and unintelligible, when it wants to be
more than a barren woman raking
the lake into fits of momentary white.

I dreamt of scarves in turquoise and fuchsia
that said here, here is joy in focus,
and wakened later to you
coming inside from the morning's blue chill
to say that deer ate the red tulips
in the dark while we slept.

The water rolls in, black with oil,
behind a man framed by my television.
He tells me "This is a casualty of war"
how there is "simply nothing to be done."
And the camera leans its weary eye
against the body of an elegant bird
smothered by the petroleum on the slick,
shiny sand.

To this creature the world was not
vicious or cruel but a blend
of natural difficulties: weather
and wind currents, sky and blue ocean,
and perhaps, on a good day, infinite fish.

So when the general, any general, says again
in his voice like brown paper, his voice
like an envelope, that the allies
have achieved "air superiority"
I want him to hear
the wings fold closed
on a thousand feathered bodies
who gave all those weaponed planes
more room
to fly.

MONFORT, COLORADO

At midday the smell of slaughter
carries into town
on the dark side of dust, heavier
than lilac or engines,
or wind blowing into cherry or plum.

At three the children tumble
from orange buses
and scatter into separate yards
to leap and holler.
By now the blood has seeped back
to the dark root
rising up through crabgrass.

When day withers to dark
the children are plucked indoors.
The men come home to their wives
with hands cracked and emptied
of light.

The women wash lard from plates,
lift their drowsy children
to bedrooms where burned hide
sifts through the screens.

After love the men disappear
down chutes of sleep.
The women see how easily flesh
slides from their bones
as they rinse and rinse
the laundry, feeling already
the tiny angry hooves
tearing through the red wall.

all things are dear that disappear.
　　　　　　—June Jordan

From the corner of my eye, a blue heron
poised on a glassy plate of water, so rare I'm startled—
two visions rise up from a week pinched by small failures:
the tiny child running across a parking lot
her small skull smooth except for a few
luminous strands of hair, her eyes bright, a triumph
over each new atrocity used to heal
her bewildered body.

And a friend's young peacock
confused by the ordinary antics
of ducks and geese
lifts himself to balance on the barn roof
a weather vane against the bruised sky.

GIVING SOMETHING BACK
after the Valdez oil spill

Because whole generations of seals,
not to mention otters, are lost,
because I can imagine the slick black
newborns sliding forth
from their mothers
greased with the oil of birth
only to be suffocated by the oil
of machinery, and because
on the ocean of sleep
I hear mother seals
howling from their dark throats
in the confusion and grief
of all mammals who lose their young
and for all the others
under the curtained surface
who still swim frantically
in search of sunlight
I give back
the garden
with its proud dry corn, whole heads
of cabbages unwrapping themselves
in the dark, the dangling jewelry of beans,
the apricots, the last sweet plums,
the brazen red cherries
all surrendered to squirrels, jays, flickers,
to the slugs, worms, and spiders
of my yard. Such a small gift
but in my dream I see again
the milky blue eyes of the sea lion
at the zoo, and how they regard
my children.

ENDANGERED SPECIES

1.
We spend a day, a century,
watching the buffalo, his massive silence
carries memories of grandmothers, fathers,
whole herds dead along the steel tracks of modern America.

Standing near the pen where giraffes
lift their small heads skyward
we suddenly smell blood in jungles,
see bellies of whales gleaming dead on a beach.

Here, between signs glaring *Endangered*
I take your picture by the chainlink fence,
enclosing wild horses and bits of paper.
You so fresh and young I forget
your bones break and life seeps
through the cloth of your body.

2.
Once, in an elevator going up,
your face illuminated in yellow light,
I knew we were a gift to each other.

And if it should ever happen,
I would press my hands to all your wounds
before letting slip this gentle rhythm
of our lives entwined,
terrified that we survive to share even this
unguarded moment.

The panic of life without you resurfaces.
I dream of a lone polar bear sleeping
on hot concrete in central Denver.

LAKE AT NIGHT

No whales tonight but the moon
sings their music, a net of light
pulling the wind
into blue slopes.

The trees, with their nests
of new leaves, move invisibly
toward shore. The air
is sharp and tangy as seaweed.

Long after dark we hear
fish rise out of the water,
their scales studded
with tiny barnacles,
their joy bigger
than their bodies.

THE DAY I WORE YOUR MOTHER'S SWEATER

Three great magpies rose
out of the cornfield
with the sun
sharp on their tails
and I felt as though
I were being marked for something
that was not bad, or good,
but simply possible.
This and your mother's death
had a weight to it
that I wore all day
under her purple cashmere
like a locket, with the small photograph
of a stranger clasped inside.

Neighbors

The man hanging clothes on the brittle line
this winter morning tells me
my horses are good neighbors.
We agree that some things
never end: hanging wash, feeding the animals.
I'm thinking how the towels and shirts will stiffen
in the chill air when he suddenly says
his wife is sick again.
The horses move around me, blowing steam.
They like the man on the hill
with his apples and his pretty wife.
He tells me her eye is swollen closed
with lymphoma. That she cannot hear
from her right ear. A sister has bought her
a ticket to Ireland, her family's homeland.
The ancestors are all buried there.
On the line the sheets catch
a whip of cold wind and stand up.
Here is where the horses need
to come back into the poem.

Where there Is No Shade

They come in their boots and gloves
chain saws screaming like nuclear insects
tearing through the trees which collapse
against one another like grieving widows.

And what you are thinking is how
in South America the forest comes down
one tree at a time, with the nests
of unnamed tropical birds crushed
within them, and small
furred creatures scurrying to make room
for cattle grazing slowly
toward their own eventual ruin.

But here, on your land,
power lines will sing
where there is no shade,
where great horned owls spent years

watching the pasture as it breathed
beneath the branches
where you are already wilting
in the hot, wingless air.

DOG FROM THE POUND

Behind the wire cage
her whole body begged down their resistance.
Impossible not to take her home,
give her a name, a new collar.

How could they know
the rampant love trapped behind her bones?
She burrowed in their blankets,
nuzzled their vacant shoes, kissed crumbs
from their empty plates.

But she could not be confined.
She thrashed against the seams of their house.
She broke from the yard, roamed down the alleys.

She would not sit or heel or stay.
They pleaded and bribed. They raised their voices.
She cowered but leaned with longing against them.
At last, unable to bear her constant forgiveness,
they gave her away.

Sometimes, along the fringe of sleep
they glimpse her running, nose to the ground,
trailing an old chain behind her in the dirt.

Something ahead on the asphalt
Dawn already gray drapery
Something ahead steaming on the asphalt
Not a paper bag fallen from—
Not paper folded heavy or a blanket drenched—
Dawn aged into morning unflaked with snow
Something breathing on the fresh
Ribbons mid-road that say don't pass
But the van ahead passes around
What lies on the iron pavement on lines bright
Painted yellow which is not
This exact morning engined
At the stop sign ahead the van
Then a car—
As if just wakened stunned between
Wired open space on either side
Her head is up looking to where
She would have been easily over the fence
Forward moment she is suddenly as if
In two pieces head and neck swiveled to see
Where she was meant to—
Something broken—
Below her shoulders on the road
Nothing moves just her head lifted
Motors edging around how
She can't get up but knows
She was leaping just then
And now plumes of breath white
Flare through her nostrils her life
all keen desire the heat of it
fogging briefly the other air

We see the land with its tidy
blocks of pasture, empty
of foxes.
Creatures are watching
as we pass. They hide inside
my dreaming which is why
we cannot see them.

Music spins inside the car
but I watch for foxes
beyond the window.
I close my eyes and their wired red bodies
leap into the insected air above
the meadow grass.

When I look again, into the real world,
we are driving past the recycling plant, night
crushed against a warehouse where hills
of radiant glass and gleaming
aluminum cans spill
from the doorway like jewels.

If This Were Egypt

Below a wet April sky John dug your grave,
the lilac blossoms above it
just small thoughts kept to themselves.

We carried your body and laid you down
in that bowl of brown earth where you curled
clean and white, a wolf, sleeping.

To take on your journey we put biscuits and cheese
and slim crocus petals which the boy
who knew you his whole life
dropped in with shaking hands.

If this were Egypt, best good dog,
we wouldn't stop there—
adding one pizza delivery guy in a red cap;
a UPS driver, the one with blond hair
springing from his head like corn straw;
the whistling meter reader you couldn't quite reach
through the wooden teeth of fence; two smart-assed
kids on mountain bikes; one young plumber
with a tool belt; the doorbell with wiring attached;
three squirrels, one grackle, a raccoon,
and, if possible, the neighbor's slinking cat.

Out of Desire Dolphins Come

1.

Everywhere under this ocean they are slipping
like petals through the waves.
In the unfinished space between the wet horizon
and the salted wind, we watch.

2.

I tell my daughter there is a living invisible world
below the boat, and we gaze out across the deceptive water,
believing that dolphins will come, even though
the day is windy, even though the day
is passing.

3.

The first dolphin lifts my body out of my body
and when other dolphins rise up for air and follow
in the frothy wake of our boat there is only this
simple ecstasy—the streamlined bodies, bellies pink
as shell, the hooked fin rising, a little flag,
into our short and stormy lives.

Lies

The sun is a broken window on fire.
The stars speak the color of my real name.
Angels whisper Osama Osama in their sleep.
The dog's bones gleam in the dark.
The dark is the underside of God's one eyelid.
Hearts are like the sun only not on fire
or do I mean not like a window
or do I mean green glass you can see through?

Truths

There is a river of grief beneath the world.
Horses remember the rumble of dinosaurs.
My boy grew an inch in less than a month.
My husband was a boy once
with a poem in his pocket.
Bales of sweet grass wear down in the barn
to give room to the cat, to give room
to the mice.
Under the lake there are turtles. Under the lake
there are mysteries. The lake knows
all about the river of grief.

WHEN WE'RE NOT WATCHING

Back at the house flies circle
lazily in the last slant of day,
the dogs hovering near the grill,
whole parts of chicken gone
when we stop watching to sip
our sparkling drinks.

But when we let the filly go,
opening the gate to pasture
thinking she'll wander off slowly, the other
horses far down the hill, suddenly
it's like a shift of wind, children standing
in the bent grass, the gelding
at a full, happy gallop bearing down
upon the smallest boy like the careless,
even accidental smack of God,
but our screams divide the pair
and the film is edited, in that spot,
at that moment, the ambulance threading
through traffic in another town
and we are not nearly grateful
enough.

MATINS

The pony and I know the wind
is coming. In the corral

on the bronze hill we do
our chores. While I rake and shovel

she follows, nudging the wheelbarrow,
ears flicking forward to listen

to the first killdeer on the lake.

I tell my husband this is my other life—
morning before the children

race for the bus, my little mare
touching my face with her soft muzzle

and frosted whiskers. When I'm gone the wind
will rush across the water and we will both be

leaning into it.

RENDERING THE LAKE

I try so hard to bead the lake
onto this thread thin as spider web.
These little seeds of silver and green
like the uncertain edge where the heron lands
in his enormous twilight of feathers.

When I look again
the sky has changed and therefore the lake,
blue and slate with swallows
dipping the black apostrophes of their wings
to the surface.

Yesterday the lake floated us in the borrowed red canoe,
and the water spread out like the rest of our lives,
sun cracking white chips everywhere around us.
What I mean is that I want to render this into earrings,
a necklace, a thing to wear against my body, here, in time.

Part Three

If, in the garden of the world,
there's such a thing as suffering
I have never suffered.
—*Richard Jones*

TURNING THE CLOCK BACK IN OCTOBER, 2001

There it is
that little clatter
of leaves unlatched from branches
ticking onto the walk

It could be what I wake to
or all the clocks' blue numbers
rattling as we shake loose an hour
the way we do every year

I am again uneasy
with this practice
wonder where that hour
hunkers down, what it does
in the dark
with its indiscriminate gang of minutes

You dream of an Afghan woman—
there is a tent, a high dry wind, sleeping children
and now this extra hour careening toward her
unsummoned, filled with cold thin teeth
and a speechless need to be used

Rural Post Office

My sister says there are countries
where postage stamps are used
as money: two stamps
for a chunk of butter, six
for a plucked chicken—
stamps for a gallon of gas, bottle of wine,
needle and thread.

Imagine a purse filled with tiny paper squares:
painted trees, cathedrals, the dictator's profile—
and a woman goes home holding
a basket of turnips, a wedge of white cheese.
If she is lucky, she will cook a hot meal
and her sons will not die
by sniper fire.

Today a guy in the post office line
needs a single stamp
but he only has a fifty dollar bill.
Almost five P.M.—the last blades of light fall
across the counter. The clerk
is tired, wants the key in the lock.
A woman steps forward,
gives the young man
the stamp with the little flag
out of her wallet.
Everybody smiles in relief
because it is late in the day

and this is North America.

If Things Were Different

There wouldn't be a puncture
in your heart or in the sky
above Antarctica.
Men and women who sit now
in the glittering quiet of waiting
would simply go home
and have supper, the test results
piled thin as ash
on the laboratory counter, each one
benign, negative, easily
cured.

And the others, like you,
who stand on a windy corner
looking down at their cuffs or watching
people cross the street into carefree lives
would see the bus shoulder the curb,
their child lighting down like an angel
on earth, this healed earth, and he's healed,
too: grown up and whole, not like
the old nightmare, no.
Not like that at all.

AFTERMATH

What was he thinking to take you to that place
seared by fire, broken by metal?
This large man, fierce in his love for you,
firstborn daughter, and you
so slim and small and blonde.

Did he lift you from the car
in one strong swoop and did you hope,
even as he settled you
onto the blackened earth
like a fragile package,
that his arms would never release you?

Such ceremony just to see the aftermath
of an airplane's fractured descent.
The bodies were removed but the bitter smoke lingered
to fill your young life. Everywhere around you
the charred ground was dotted
with dozens of forlorn and empty shoes.

What did he imagine then, your father,
standing remote and silent, like God?
And you beside him, his witness
to the soft slippered twilight gliding
as if with love between the estranged and separated pairs.

LORD BYRON'S MOTHER,
GIGHT CASTLE, SCOTLAND

He might not come. She knows this as she feels
winter's glove slipping over her,
the rooms in the castle cold
without him to stir the fires.
Night brings its own small rain.

She does not know how tired she is
does not know I am here
two hundred years later
feeling her waiting, listening
for the horse's stormy breath, hoofs striking
flint on the slope up.

How many nights rose and fell
before comfort gave way to truth and rain wore down
the stones of this hearth?

Look at the river, still ignorant,
carving its slow way between hills
below the terrace.
Look at the tree growing now in the dining room
where she might have lifted a glass and laughed,
not seeing the ruin to come, the slow unwinding
in her body.

OKLAHOMA, 1885

Her brown hand shades her eyes
but there is only the meadowlark, out of nowhere,
all the other women so far away
their voices are nothing to this wind
beating the one tree down into prayer.

Sod house and no way to keep the centipedes
and small snakes from the walls so she stands
out on what would be a front stoop
while day travels toward her as heat
rising over the barren field.

On this terrain the rivers are only rumor,
the gullies beneath full of wasted hope
creased and rippled as an unmade bed.
Tips of yellow grass lead to her house
the door a mouth gaping.
Hot wind blows the clouds north
and all the while kicks the milk pail dry.
I was so lonely I carried a beetle in my apron pocket
all day, to and fro to and fro.

ANNE B.

Nobody would ever accuse her
of getting in over her head.
And head over heels? Not this girl.
The king is an idiot but she knows
what's what. His anger
is a monster full of phlegm
and envy. She keeps him
well fed and sweetly
tended.
The midwives give her herbs
she holds in secret.
The tiny queen grows inside her
like a new planet.
When her husband grunts and farts
in his fattened sleep
she sits beside the window
and looks out across the embroidered fields.
Sometimes she is not even cold,
not even afraid.

HUNTED

At night a harvest moon
bleaches the road,
streaming between low hills.
It lights up the train
thundering past the Cottonwood Motel
where love is a collision and deep sleep.

Beneath the blinking sign
a woman moves against a man.
She feels the rattled glass
up through the window of her pelvis

to her heart which falls
in a scattering of feathers
warm and plumed in the field.

SINGING

My mother, a small blonde wisp, circling her mother's chair
in the doctor's office. Round and round, the little warble sweetening
the antiseptic air. My grandmother, young, dark, poor, and embarrassed,
tells her child hush. The doctor, the doctor is always sad.
It is The Great Depression and he looks hard into the face
of everyone's hunger. "Mrs. Raeburn," he says quietly.
"Never tell a child to stop singing."

DREAMING

My sister dreamed about our mother often after she died.
I admit it, I was jealous. But when my mother finally spoke to me
from behind some gray curtain, as if she were backstage, it was to criticize.
"Have you slept with him?" she asked, already judging, already furious.
"Yes," I said. "Yes." In the dream and in my heart,
the meadowlark was just beginning.

ODE TO THE WHITE SHIRT
for John

What is it about a man
in a white shirt?
Is it the clean starched shroud
drifting across the wings of his collarbone?
Or is it the infantry of buttons tucked
into their own pockets, their march
in a line from the fragile throat,
crossing the sternum's valiant terrain,
over the belly a woman loves
for itself, but the man hates
for its signs of age.

It could be the way shirttails have to be urged
into the man's trousers, that little leap and tug
of the zipper which women hide from their lovers,
but men do quickly, thinking about work,
about getting into the car.

When a man slips the bleached cotton
over his own skin, skin with the shower's
fresh soap just lifting
the woman who loves him leans briefly
against the delicate, strong stitches and thinks
O pale shirt of tranquility and daylight
you know how this man is made,
and the long, steady hours
of a working day.

The Exiled Poet Reads to a Mostly Middle Class White Audience

> *The white page is pure amnesia.*
> —Bei Dao

When the Chinese poet
read his poems in his original tongue

symbols turned in his mouth
dissolved into words, little

singing sounds
flew around his face

like papery moths saved
from a burning decade

and into the audience
small black brooms swept

between two centuries
a child's hands

letting go a few, a hundred,
numberless silk stars.

MISCARRIAGE
for M.

It comes back to this slate sky
bloated yet empty, but for the sun
a cough of light above the horizon.

What gives meaning to the day?
The last apples fall on leaves
layering hardened ground.
You hear everything arrive
against the silence:
dawn, midday, evening.

At home you lower your body
like worn cloth, into the bath.
Nothing marks the wound
as night drapes the house
and sheep slumber in the field
across the road.
But a girl is there
moving among them
and her name leaps like a small fish
in your dream, a single candle
in the dark.

AFTER THE LETTER ARRIVES
for Alf, 1926–1991

Somewhere far from this place he is going,
from the lungs outward, an exhalation
of just so many years.
Here where I live I walk along a lake
where my dog is a white ghost in the weeds
and the moon bends down, washing the water.
On his island it's not dark at all, but morning
maybe rain gray above the smokestacks
and he is bringing me breakfast in that tiny house,
up the narrow stairs, over and over again—
milk spilled in the saucer but the tea still hot
with toast swirling its own private steam
and I am still waking up to it all as he leaves.

Nowhere Near a Meadow

There is no heart in a war.
The gods sit elsewhere
playing marbles, humming.
While on earth in some 4th world country
the hinge of despair flames into gunfire
along brick buildings, schoolchildren crouched
beside a wall like fallen blossoms,
machine gun shells scattered across the burning streets.

MAGICIAN

How the hand lifts and opens,
white dove escaping
into the sulphurous spotlight.
How did he hide the motion of her wings
for so long?
Enchanting us with filmy scarves,
a lit cigarette from nowhere, smoking.
It is the sweetest deception.
He flicks his wrist: a fan of cards
appears and vanishes.
He rolls his sleeves, reveals bare arms,
claps his hands and releases
another unruffled bird who flies up
into the breathless thin air
of our believing.

Snorkeling Off the Isla Mujeres

There are no warnings
where the earth falls away,
the sudden slope under.

I assume fins, awkward until
the wet edge takes me in and down
to the reef, living rock
where blue minnows dart and flash
and the angels have eyes
that never close.

I want to live here
in this world without sin,
without seasons, eternity in motion
where light angles through water
where nothing is safe but all things
are sacred.

I wish for gills.
Here, arguments are wordless,
death is soundless and arrives
on the white sand
of the Island of Women
washed of blood and remorse,
hollowed iridescent bone
with the distant roar of ocean
caught inside.

WEDDING PHOTOGRAPHER, DENVER, 1995

for Bill Wiley

Even this early the church is hot,
the stained glass face of Christ
looks damp from below
where the photographer stands
behind his camera on its high pedestal.
He is waiting, tall and patient, for the bride and groom
to ease into focus.
Beneath the altar a small fan spins
tufts of God's air
into the room, into the past
where a boy sits leggy and silent
in the hot summer liquid
of his upstairs bedroom. He is watching
the neighbor's cat cross the empty
weedy field beyond the window
and you feel how it is, the slow
lifted shoulders of them both
the irrelevant weight of binoculars
in the boy's hands,
the quiet rapture of hours falling down,
down into the evening grass.

Late Elegy

It's hard to use suffering in a poem
if you live in the United States
where pipes pour hot water into drains
that fall through more pipes beneath the house.
I could say the new spears of daffodil suffer
under these eight inches of snow
but it's a lie.
And the wind unraveling ice into lace
at the lake's edge
is no tragedy.
I could say my mother was beautiful at twenty
and a beautiful ruin by forty.
How she wrung the bottle's neck for consolation.
Five years since a blood flower petaled
and pooled in her head.
Far from here snow on her grave
drifts lightly against
the small letters of her name
suffered into granite.

December Scripture

Not an altogether fluid season,
consumer noise pinched bitter in town
that parenthesis we've answered
beyond gnashed steel and cement
the clicking road where cars
scrape the gravel questions.
I'm trying to say with this glacial string
of kicked syllables how glad I am
to live with you outside the built world
along instead the field's knee deep yellow tide,
the lake's wet imagination.

Early Valentine

The cornfields undress beneath snow
and the dog would sing at the end of his leash
if he weren't a dog.
Our hands fold together
while our boots crunch ice
under a smoke blue sky.
I am holding this whole world in my heart, love,
the words for it just a sweet dust
on my tongue.

THE NEW YEAR

I have a daughter who told me
a woman is raped
every six seconds.
Every fifteen seconds a person
dies of AIDS. She is informed
by television. She didn't ask me
if I can live with it: the t.v.
or the news it delivers—
a hundred and fifty thousand soldiers
sleeping toward Iraq, a country
sleeping toward a war.

A friend said, "I did not come
into this life joyful. I came in
motivated." Here is a woman
who knows how to find
her own happiness.
As for me, I swim back,
remember long hours
of desperate quiet,
my drunken mother,
the house slumbering
in the middle of the street,
how I came in, if anything,
reverent.

Now I can just about manage
this winter wind
leaping through the barn door
right behind me,
willful and determined.
I row hard against the sadness.
My mares follow their flakes of hay
across the corral
but they do it slowly, knowing
each patch of grass will land
like last summer's postcard
onto the beaten earth.

At the End of September

The wind's leafy incense moves
over the soaked ground, feathers
through my horse's mane as she stands
in the woven dusk on this curve of earth.
So much green still reaching up
through musky undergrowth—
geese scratching their black letter overhead.
Dawn is arriving on another landscape
as an explosion of light and shrapnel.
Night bends her spine over the mountains
in front of me, the day's static finally asleep
in the weeds.

TOO MUCH TIME ON MY HANDS

I'm afraid of snow inside my cells.
One spring it rained and rained
horses stood in mud
ankle deep, hours
steamed into weeks.
I'm afraid of colic, the invisible
twist of intestine,
rain streaked their backs
their long silk faces.
I'm afraid of extinction, coral reefs
reduced to ash in the salt tide.
When the phone rings past midnight
I am warned into waking.
I'm afraid of nuclear war, nuclear winter,
widowed at fifty, losing my keys,
lightning close to the house
that fizz of electricity, the dog limping,
the spiral of forgetting.
I'm afraid of cancer,
years of drought, not remembering
the good sun entering the barn
on an ordinary
dreamy day.

DAWNING

Some time now
since a boy wakened
and wandered in thin pajamas
to this bedroom
to let go of his repeating nightmare
and lie quietly
down on the sheets,
a slim, shivering bookmark
between the pages
of our sleepy love.
These nights I'm the one waking,
head filled with too much
of each day undone
or not enough of tasting
one whole hour in my mouth
and knowing it.
Tonight I remember
to praise the drifting moon
for giving your shoulder
its muscled curve,
to thank, in advance,
the morning which faith
tells me will arrive
with all its brave hope intact,
a splash of yellow finches
singing against
the vanishing dark.

LISA ZIMMERMAN was educated at Colorado State University and Washington University in St. Louis where she received her M.F.A. Her poems and short fiction have appeared in many journals including *Atlanta Review*, *Colorado Review*, *The Sun*, *Indiana Review*, *River Styx* and *Many Mountains Moving*. In 1986 she won Redbook magazine's short fiction contest. She has published two chapbooks, most recently *Traveling Among the Animals* (Pudding House Publications, 2002). In 2003 she had poetry nominated for a Pushcart Prize. She lives in Fort Collins, Colorado with her husband and family and teaches writing at the University of Northern Colorado in Greeley.

ACKNOWLEDGMENTS

Thanks to the editors of the magazines and anthologies who first published these poems, some in slightly different form:

"If This Were Egypt," *Atlanta Review*; "How a Sliver of Purple Far Away Became My Daughter Running Toward Me," *The Bridge*; "If Things Were Different," "Photo of the Fireman and the Child," Rendering the Lake," "The Exiled Poet Reads to a Mostly Middle Class White Audience," and "Arthur and His Sister," *California State Poetry Quarterly*; "Middle Child," *Chachalaca Poetry Review*; "Witnesses," *Colorado North Review*; "When We're Not Watching," *Colorado Review*; "Snorkeling Off the Isla Mujeres," *Descant*; "How I See It," and "Persian Gulf, January 25, 1991," *Florida Review*; "Monfort, Colorado," and "Aftermath," *Germination*; "Singing/Dreaming," "Ode to the White Shirt," *Heliotrope*; "On the Beach, Cancun," "Marketplace," and "Magician," *Hudson Valley Echoes*; "Night Light," and "Miscarriage," *Iowa Woman*; "Where There Is No Shade," *Journal of Progressive Human Services*; "Oklahoma, 1885," and "Hunted," *Mañana*; "Lake at Night," "The Wind, the Lake, the Deer," *Many Mountains Moving*; "Neighbors," *Mediphors*; "Endangered Species," *Nebo*; "The Night After the Partial Eclipse," *New Rag Rising*; "When God Made the Baby," *Owen Wister Review*; "Dog from the Pound," *Palo Alto Review*; "Lies/Truths," and "What Is the Weight of a Boy's Grief?" *Poemmemoirstory*; "Out of Desire Dolphins Come," *Prayers to Protest: Poems that Center and Bless Us*; "Matins," *Salt Hill Journal*; "How the Garden Looks from Here," *Santa Fe Sun*; "After the Letter Arrives," *STET*; "Past Lives," "Sewing Batman's Cape After the Funeral of a Friend's Son," "Avalon and the Dinosaurs," and "The Wash Prayer," *The Sun*; "Giving Something Back," *Voices, the Art and Science of Psychotherapy*.

"Early Valentine" appeared on Fort Collins City Buses in 2003 as part of the *Poetry in Motion* project.

Grateful acknowledgment to Pudding House Publications for publishing a number of these poems in my chapbook *Traveling Among the Animals*.

How The Garden Looks From Here is the winner of the 2004
Violet Reed Haas Prize for Poetry
      Judge: Rick Campbell

Previous Winners:

Tania Rochelle for *Karaoke Funeral*
      Judge: Marty L. Williams

Penelope Scambly Schott for *The Perfect Mother*
      Judge: Van K. Brock

Barbara Goldberg for *Marvelous Pursuits*
      Juge: David Kirby

Seaborn Jones for *Lost Keys*
      Judge: Robert Earl Price

Judith Hemschemeyer for *Certain Animals*
      Judge: Judson Mitchum